by Scott
Sonneborn

ATTACK OF THE INVISIBLE CATS

**illustrated by
Art Baltazar**

Superman created by
Jerry Siegel and Joe Shuster
by special arrangement with the Jerry Siegel family

raintree
a Capstone company — publishers for children

Starring...

KRYPTO
THE SUPER-DOG

THE
SPACE CANINE
PATROL AGENTS

THE
PHANTY-
CATS

CONTENTS

SUPER-PET HERO FILE 012:
SPACE CANINE PATROL AGENTS

CHAMELEON COLLIE
Power: shape-shifting

TUSKY HUSKY
Power: giant tusk

KRYPTO (LEADER)
Powers: flight, heat vision,
X-ray vision, super-speed,
super-strength, super-breath

PAW POOCH
Power: multiple paws

BULL DOG
Power: horns

TAIL TERRIER
Power: elastic tail

MAMMOTH MUTT
Power: super-growth

HOT DOG
Power: fire

Bio: A powerful pack of pooches, the Space Canine Patrol
Agents (SCPA) obey the message of their sacred oath:
"Big dog! Big dog! Bow-wow-wow! We'll crush evil! Now, now, now!"

SUPER-PET ENEMY FILE 012:
PHANTY-CATS

GENERAL MANX   **NIZZ**   **FER-EL**

SUPER-VILLAIN OWNER FILE 012:
PHANTOM ZONE CRIMINALS

GENERAL ZOD   **URSA**   **NON**

Chapter 1

DOG DAYS

It was a beautiful day on Geegax.

The planet's two purple Suns beamed

brightly in the clear, orange sky.

The president of Geegax stood on

a stage in the planet's biggest park.

"Today," she said, "we honour the

Space Canine Patrol Agents."

Everyone in the crowd cheered.

"Each of these amazing dogs has a different superpower," continued the president. "Together, they use their powers to protect Geegax and the rest of the galaxy from evil cats. Would you like to meet them?"

"Yes!" the crowd roared.

The president turned to the curtain behind her. "Come on out, friends!" she called.

WHOOSH!

A dog flew out from behind the curtain. He wore a red cape and had a friendly smile.

"**Krypto**," said the president. "Leader of the Space Canine Patrol Agents."

Two more dogs followed Krypto on to the stage. The president pointed at them. "**Chameleon Collie** can change his shape into anything he wants," she continued. "**Mammoth Mutt** can grow six metres tall."

"I can get even bigger than that," said Mammoth Mutt. "Just watch."

Mammoth Mutt grew and grew! As she did, her fur began to shed. Soon, dog hair covered the entire stage.

"Not again," said Chameleon Collie, embarrassed by the mess.

The bashful bow-wow turned himself into a rug. He hoped no one would notice him in the pile of hair.

"And here come Hot Dog and Tusky Husky," the president said.

ZOOM!

Two more dogs burst on to the

stage. **Hot Dog** bowed and created a

beautiful streak of fire. **Tusky Husky**

showed off his giant tusk.

More dogs trotted on to the stage.

One had horns like a bull. The other

had twenty paws. "Welcome,

Bull Dog and **Paw Pooch**,"

the president said.

The planet's leader looked around.

"Where is the last member of the

Space Canine Patrol Agency?" she

asked. "Where is Tail Terrier?"

"I'm sure I can find him," Krypto

said with a smile. He lifted his ears

and listened with his super-hearing.

"CHLA-SNOOO!"
"CHLA-SNOOO!"

The Super-Dog heard snoring.

"There he is!" Krypto said. He used
his X-ray vision to see backstage. Sure
enough, **Tail Terrier** was snoring
away. The old dog had fallen asleep
while waiting for his turn!

After a moment, Tail Terrier finally made his way on to the stage. Then the president turned to the eight dogs of the **Space Canine Patrol Agency.** "Thank you for keeping the galaxy safe from evil cats!" she said.

"In honour of your good deeds," continued the president, "the people of Geegax would like to present you with this special award."

The president held up a gold trophy. It was shaped like a giant dog bone.

"ACHOOOOOOOOO!"

Paw Pooch let out a powerful sneeze.

"What's the matter?" Mammoth

Mutt asked him. "Allergic to bones?"

"Nope," replied Paw Pooch, wiping

his snout. "I'm only allergic to cats."

"Impossible," said the president. "There are no cats on Geegax."

She was wrong. At that moment, three cats stood only a few metres away. The president did not see them. No one did. They were invisible!

Their names were **General Manx, Nizz, and Fer-El**, but they were better known throughout the galaxy as...

For years, these feline felons had robbed dozens of planets.

Recently, the Space Canine Patrol Agency had captured the kitties and placed them in the **Phantom Zone**. This space prison held hundreds of criminals. The Phanty-Cats were now among the few that had ever escaped.

General Manx had discovered a way out of their jail, and the three had made a run for it. Once they were free, the trio created a potion to make themselves invisible. They planned to get back at Krypto, the dog who had captured them in the first place.

"We will get our revenge!" whispered

Fer-El. "Isn't that right, General?"

General Manx nodded his invisible

head. "Those mutts have ruined our

kitty capers too many times," he said.

"Now, we'll ruin their dog day!"

On the far side of the stage, a band was playing. No one heard the invisible cats beneath the platform.

The feline felons began quietly pulling apart the wooden beams under the band. Soon, that part of the stage would break. The band would tumble into the crowd.

"ACHOOOOO!"

On the other side of the stage, Paw Pooch sneezed again. **"I'm telling you, there are cats here,"** he said.

No one could see the invisible cats. Thanks to some powerful noses, though, the Space Canine Patrol Agents could smell them.

"You're right," Krypto said. **"I smell three cats under the stage."**

"I smell them, too, but I still don't see them," said Hot Dog.

"There are only three cats in the galaxy with big enough brains to turn invisible –" Krypto began.

"The Phanty-Cats!" cried Tail Terrier.

At that moment, the stage started to wobble. Band members lost their balance and tumbled down off the side. Mammoth Mutt and the other Space Canines rushed to catch them.

"What's that?" asked the president.

"Invisible cats!" shouted Krypto. He flew to help the other dogs.

Of course, none of the Geegaxians saw the invisible cats. They only saw the Space Canines causing the mess.

The Phanty-Cats' plan was working!

Krypto tried to explain that the Phanty-Cats were to blame, but the Geegaxians did not believe him.

"Invisible cats?" said the president. "I've never heard of such a thing!"

Chameleon Collie was embarrassed. He turned himself into a rock and rolled under the stage.

PURRFECT PLAN

The president asked the crowd to settle down. "The carnival and the feast will go on," she said. Then the president turned to Krypto. "There won't be any more trouble, will there?"

"No, I promise," said Krypto.

Krypto turned to the other dogs. "We will stop the Phanty-Cats before they can cause any more harm, won't we?"

The pooches chanted their battle cry: **"Big dog! Big dog! Bow-wow-wow! We'll crush evil! Now, now, now!"**

Then Krypto split the team up into two. "You four go to the feast," he told Tusky Husky, Tail Terrier, Mammoth Mutt, and Paw Pooch. **"The rest of us will protect the carnival."**

WHOOSH!

Soon, half the Space Canines

arrived at the feast. Dozens of tables

were piled with strange foods, such as

square bananas and cabbage cheese.

"Look at these tasty treats!" said

Tusky Husky, trying not to slobber.

"We're not here to eat," Tail Terrier reminded Tusky. **"We're on patrol."**

Mammoth Mutt nodded. "Keep your noses open for any sign of those Phanty-Cats," she barked. The dogs lifted their snouts in the air.

"All I smell is delicious food," moaned Tusky.

"Achoo!" sneezed Paw Pooch. "I smell something else. There's a Phanty-Cat here. Right under that table!"

Paw Pooch reached out with a dozen paws to grab Nizz. The cat skittered out from the other side.

As she ran, the furry feline bumped into tables. Bowls of sauce and plates of beans spilled all over the floor.

"Stop her!" cried Paw Pooch.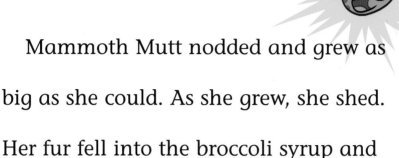

Mammoth Mutt nodded and grew as big as she could. As she grew, she shed. Her fur fell into the broccoli syrup and the pitchers of meat juice.

Seeing Mammoth Mutt blocking the door, Nizz stopped short. Tail Terrier whipped out his tail to grab her, but Nizz ducked. His tail hit a table and splattered marshmallow gravy all over the floor.

KA-SPLAT!

Nizz turned and scrambled over to a window. Tusky Husky leapt at her. He missed and landed on a buffet.

THUD! The food flew everywhere!

As Nizz skittered out of the window, the dogs raced to follow. Then one of the Geegaxians shouted, "Stop right there! Where do you think you're going? You just ruined our feast."

None of the Geegaxians had seen the invisible cat. They only saw the Space Canines running wild.

Tail Terrier sighed. "I hope Krypto and the others are having better luck at the carnival," he said.

They were not.

At that very moment, Krypto, Bull Dog, Chameleon Collie, and Hot Dog were following the scent of Fer-El and General Manx around the carnival.

As the invisible cats darted under the roller coaster, Bull Dog charged after them. His horns hit the ride, and it started to sway.

The roller coaster teetered over the carnival's giant swimming pool. Krypto and Chameleon Collie rushed to get everyone off the ride. Hot Dog cornered the cats with his snout.

"One move and you're toast!" said Hot Dog, holding up a flaming paw.

The roller coaster fell into the pool. Everyone at the carnival got soaked, including Hot Dog. His flame went out, and the Phanty-Cats raced away.

"I can explain –" Krypto started to tell the president.

"I don't want to hear any more stories about invisible cats," roared the president. "You've ruined our carnival and our feast. This celebration is over!"

The president took the golden bone trophy and walked away.

"Wait! Where are you going?" asked Krypto.

"To send a message to the presidents of all the other planets," she replied. "I want them to know that the Space Canine Patrol Agents are nothing but a bunch of troublemakers! You won't be welcome anywhere in the galaxy!"

Chapter 3

THE HAIRY END

As the president walked away, Krypto knew there was only one thing to do. "You have to give us that golden bone," Krypto told her.

The president turned back to the Space Canine Patrol Agents. "Why would I do that?" she asked.

"The Phanty-Cats are the ones who ruined the celebration," replied the Super-Dog. "I think they'll turn up at the golden bone ceremony, too. **When they do, we'll catch them.**"

"I still don't believe there are any cats at all," huffed the president.

"We can prove it," said Krypto. "If my plan doesn't work, I promise we'll leave and never come back."

"Okay," the president agreed. "I'll give you one more chance."

Minutes later, the president walked on to the stage to start the ceremony. Not a single Geegaxian had attended the event. They were cross with the Space Canines. No one wanted to see them get their golden trophy.

Chameleon Collie was more embarrassed than ever. He changed into a chair and hid behind a table.

Sitting on the empty lawn, the three invisible cats smiled. Their plan was working perfectly. **"Give me a high-five,"** purred Nizz.

Nizz held up her paw. General Manx tried to smack the invisible paw, but hit Nizz's face instead. **THWAP!**

"**Owww!**" hissed Nizz.

"Sorry," said the General. "It's hard to high-five when you're invisible."

"Achoo!" Paw Pooch sneezed.

Krypto lifted his nose and sniffed the air. "The Phanty-Cats are here," he whispered.

"Where?" grumbled the president. "I still don't see any cats."

"You will," replied Krypto. "Do your thing, Mammoth Mutt!"

The Space Canine nodded. Then she started to grow. As Mammoth Mutt got bigger, she shed and shed and shed some more!

Mammoth Mutt continued to grow. Fur fell all over the stage, the other dogs, and the president.

"You're getting dog hair all over my dress!" cried the president. "How is this helping?"

"Just wait," said Krypto, smiling.

As the dog hair landed, it also fell on to the invisible cats. Covered in dog hair, the cats were now easy to see.

"You were right!" exclaimed the president. "There *are* three cats here."

"Not for long!" cried Bull Dog as he rushed over to them.

"Run!" yelled Nizz.

The cats bolted. Hot Dog fired a heat blast at Nizz. The cat jumped aside and hid behind a small chair.

"Where'd she go?" asked Hot Dog.

Nizz smiled. Just as she was about to slink away, the chair grabbed her. It was Chameleon Collie!

Meanwhile, Tusky Husky chased Fer-El and General Manx. They raced ahead and ducked around a corner.

Just then, Fer-El saw a green ball of string on the ground. Fer-El and General Manx may have been evil, but they *were* still cats. They could not help but play with the string.

Fer-El reached out to bat it with his paw, but it pulled away. He chased it around the corner and General Manx followed. Then they realized the long string was not a string at all.

It was Tail Terrier's tail!

The crooked cats were surprised. So surprised, in fact, that they did not see Paw Pooch until he had them wrapped tightly in all twenty of his legs.

Krypto pulled out his trusty Pocket Phantom Zone Projector. It sent the evil-doers back to the Phantom Zone. **They were in prison once again!**

The president ran up to the Space Canine Patrol Agents. She thanked them and gave them the golden bone. "I'm sorry I didn't believe you before," she said.

"That's okay," said Krypto. "I knew you would once Mammoth Mutt *shed* a little light on the situation!"

"Ow!" howled Chameleon Collie. He turned into a rock and rolled away, embarrassed by Krypto's bad joke.

KNOW YOUR HERO PETS

1. Krypto
2. Streaky
3. Beppo
4. Comet
5. Ace
6. Robin Robin
7. Jumpa
8. Whatzit
9. Storm
10. Topo
11. Ark
12. Hoppy
13. Batcow
14. Big Ted
15. Proty
16. Gleek
17. Paw Pooch
18. Bull Dog
19. Chameleon Collie
20. Hot Dog
21. Tail Terrier
22. Tusky Husky
23. Mammoth Mutt
24. Dawg
25. B'dg
26. Stripezoid
27. Zallion
28. Ribitz
29. Bzzd
30. Gratch
31. Buzzoo
32. Fossfur
33. Zhoomp
34. Eeny

 1

 2

 3

 4

 5

 6

 7

 8

 9

 10

 11

 12

 13

 14

 15

 16

 17

 18

 19

 20

 21

 22

 23

 24

 25

 26

 27

 28

 29

 30

 31

 32

33

 34

KNOW YOUR VILLAIN PETS

1. Bizarro Krypto
2. Ignatius
3. Rozz
4. Mechanikat
5. Crackers
6. Giggles
7. Joker Fish
8. Chauncey
9. Artie Puffin
10. Griff
11. Waddles
12. Dogwood
13. Mr. Mind
14. Sobek
15. Misty
16. Sneezers
17. General Manx
18. Nizz
19. Fer-El
20. Titano
21. Bit-Bit
22. X-43
23. Dex-Starr
24. Glomulus
25. Whoosh
26. Pronto
27. Snorrt
28. Rolf
29. Tootz
30. Eezix
31. Donald
32. Waxxee
33. Fimble
34. Webbik

1

2

3

4

5

6

7

8

9

10

11

12

13

14

15

16

17

18

19

20

21

22

23

24

25

26

27

28

29

30

31

32

33

34

JOKES

What is a cat's favourite colour?

Dunno.

Purr-ple!

Why do dogs run in circles?

I give up.

Because it is so hard to run in squares!

How is a dog like a penny?

Tell me.

They both have heads and tails!

GLOSSARY

allergic having an unpleasant reaction – such as sneezing or breaking out in a rash – to a substance

bashful shy and easily embarrassed

caper silly or naughty act

ceremony event to mark an important occasion

embarrassed feeling awkward or uncomfortable

felon someone who has committed a crime

galaxy large group of stars and planets

MEET THE AUTHOR

Scott Sonneborn

Scott Sonneborn has written dozens of books, one circus (for Ringling Bros. Barnum & Bailey), and several television programmes. He has been nominated for one Emmy and spent three very cool years working at DC Comics. He lives with his wife and their two sons.

MEET THE ILLUSTRATOR

Eisner Award-winner Art Baltazar

Art Baltazar defines cartoons and comics not only as a style of art, but as a way of life. Art is the creative force behind *The New York Times* best-selling, Eisner Award-winning, DC Comics series Tiny Titans, and the co-writer for *Billy Batson and the Magic of SHAZAM!* Art draws comics and never has to leave the house. He lives with his lovely wife, Rose, big boy Sonny, little boy Gordon, and little girl Audrey.

ART BALTAZAR
says:

Read all the DC SUPER-PETS stories today!

ATTACK OF THE INVISIBLE CATS

BACKWARD BOWWOW

BATTLE BUGS OF OUTER SPACE

THE FASTEST PET ON EARTH

HEROES OF THE HIGH SEAS

THE HOPPING HERO

MONKEY MADNESS

POOCHES OF POWER!

ROYAL RODENT RESCUE

SALAMANDER SMACKDOWN

SUPER HERO SPLASH DOWN

SUPERPOWERED PONY

Raintree is an imprint of Capstone Global Library Limited, a company
incorporated in England and Wales having its registered office at 264 Banbury
Road, Oxford, OX2 7DY – Registered company number: 6695582

www.raintree.co.uk
myorders@raintree.co.uk

First published by Picture Window Books in 2012
First published in the United Kingdom in 2012
The moral rights of the proprietor have been asserted.

Art Director and Designer: Bob Lentz
Editors: Donald Lemke and Vaarunika Dharmapala
Creative Director: Heather Kindseth
Editorial Director: Michael Dahl

ISBN 978 1 4747 6445 2 (paperback)
21 20 19 18 17
10 9 8 7 6 5 4 3 2 1

British Library Cataloguing in Publication Data
A full catalogue record for this book is available from the British Library.

Printed and bound in India